Izzy
Barr,
Running
Star

Franklin School Friends

Izzy Barr, Running Star

Claudia Mills

pictures by Rob Shepperson

Margaret Ferguson Books

Farrar Straus Giroux • New York

Farrar Straus Giroux Books for Young Readers
175 Fifth Avenue, New York 10010

Printed in the United States of America by R. R. Donnelley & Sons
Company, Harrisonburg, Virginia
First edition, 2015
1 3 5 7 9 10 8 6 4 2

mackids.com

Library of Congress Cataloging-in-Publication Data
Mills, Claudia.
    Izzy Barr, running star / Claudia Mills ; pictures by Rob Shepperson.
—First edition.
        pages cm — (Franklin School friends)
    "Margaret Ferguson books."
    Summary: "The third book in the Franklin School Friends series
is a fast and funny story about sports, friendship, and sibling rivalries"
—Provided by publisher.
    ISBN 978-0-374-33578-6 (hardback)
    ISBN 978-0-374-33579-3 (e-book)
    [1. Schools—Fiction.   2. Friendship—Fiction.]   I. Shepperson, Rob,
illustrator.   II. Title.

PZ7.M63963Iz 2015
[Fic]—dc23
                                                    2014023488

Farrar Straus Giroux Books for Young Readers may be purchased
for business or promotional use. For information on bulk purchases
please contact Macmillan Corporate and Premium Sales Department at
(800) 221-7945 x5442 or by email at specialmarkets@macmillan.com.

Izzy
Barr,
Running
Star

1

Izzy Barr retied the laces on her running shoes. Once the laces were nice and tight, she finished her jumping jacks. Mr. Tipton, the Franklin School P.E. teacher, wouldn't let Mrs. Molina's third graders start running until they had done some exercises to warm up. Izzy knew this was important, but it was hard to wait.

"All right, Miss Izzy," Mr. Tipton finally told her, grinning. "All right, everybody. Now it's time to run."

Izzy took off around the track that rimmed the school's athletic field. Two of the boys in her third-grade class—Simon Ellis and Cody Harmon—were only a bit behind her. Izzy's two best friends, Kelsey Green and Annika Riz, were way behind them. Kelsey loved reading, not running. Annika loved math, not running. But in Izzy's opinion, everyone should love running—or at least like running—especially on this cool Friday morning in May, with its gentle breezes urging them on: *Faster! Faster!*

Then someone pulled ahead of Izzy. It was the only person in Izzy's class—girl or boy—who was faster than she was: Skipper Tipton.

Skipper *Tipton*: Mr. Tipton's daughter.

Izzy picked up her pace.

Skipper picked up her pace, too.

Finally, on the last stretch of the school track, Izzy pulled ahead of Skipper.

They finished the lap with Izzy just one step ahead.

Whew!

Maybe Izzy would be the fastest runner on third-grade Field Day at the end of next week. And then maybe she'd be the fastest kid her age in the citywide 10K race held on Memorial Day, just three days after Field Day. A 10K race was long—*10K* meant 10 kilometers, which meant 6.2 miles—but not as long as a whole 26.2-mile marathon. Still, definitely a very long way.

Izzy had been training hard for the 10K race for almost two months now in the Franklin School Fitness Club, coached by Mr. Tipton, as well as doing longer runs on the weekend at home. But Skipper Tipton was training hard with the Fitness Club, too. And she had a P.E. teacher and running coach as her father.

Izzy's father wasn't a teacher or a runner; he was a foreman in a factory just outside of town. And sometimes he didn't even come to her races or softball games because he was too busy attending the sports events of her half brother,

Dustin. If only her dad would come to Field Day *and* the 10K race to see her cross the finish line *both* times first—ahead of Miss Skipper Tipton!

At least Izzy had come in first today. She couldn't keep herself from grinning.

As if to show how little she cared, Skipper tossed her long blond ponytail.

Then Skipper's face brightened with satisfaction as she stooped down and made a big show of retying the laces on her shoes.

Izzy stared at Skipper's feet. "You got new shoes!"

Skipper's new shoes were the coolest, most beautiful model of running shoes: bright blue with silver arrows along the sides. Izzy had wanted a pair exactly like them forever.

"They cost a hundred dollars," Skipper said. "My dad bought them for me last night at the mall. He said they'll make me run even faster."

Izzy looked down at her old, scuffed running

shoes. Well, they weren't that old or that scuffed. But they were discount-store shoes bought on sale. They were dingy gray, not bright blue. They didn't have any silver arrows.

"Your new shoes didn't make you run faster today," Izzy couldn't resist pointing out.

"They're not broken in yet," Skipper said. "But they'll be broken in by Field Day. And definitely in time for the 10K race."

Skipper smiled smugly and retied her already perfectly tied laces one more time.

Annika and Kelsey finished their laps, walking at the end, not running. Izzy was grateful to have an excuse to leave Skipper and go over to join them.

"Skipper has brand-new running shoes," Izzy told her friends as they plopped down on the grass to rest before practicing some of the other Field Day events: long jump, high jump, softball throw. On Field Day there would be other just-for-fun things, like a goofy race with kids bouncing along on huge hoppy balls, but Mr. Tipton didn't have the kids practice for those.

"You're still a better runner than she is," Kelsey said, pushing her straight brown hair back from her face.

It wasn't true, but Izzy was glad Kelsey had said it.

Annika fanned herself with the end of one of her long blond braids. Annika's hair was even longer than Skipper's. "I bet she'll brag about her shoes all the time," Annika said.

That *was* true.

"Look at Mr. Boone!" Kelsey said then.

Izzy could hardly believe her eyes. Finishing the lap around the track last of all was their school principal.

He must have joined the lap partway through; Izzy hadn't seen him at the start of the run. Mr. Boone was chubby, and he was wearing his regular principal clothes—suit and tie—so he looked silly puffing along behind everyone else. But Mr. Boone never minded looking silly. He had shaved off his big, bushy beard once for a school reading contest. He had let himself be dunked twenty-seven times at the school carnival. Now he was pretending to train for Field Day.

When he puffed across the finish line, far behind even the slowest students, he clasped his hands together and raised them high in a victory cheer.

The kids all laughed. Everyone loved Mr. Boone.

"Keep—on—running!" Mr. Boone gasped. Izzy knew he was acting more winded than he actually was. He mopped his brow with his handkerchief. "Go—Mrs.—Molina's—third—graders!"

Then, giving a final wave, he jogged off slowly toward the school building, his tie flapping.

Izzy planned to keep on running, even with her old, uncool shoes.

The only trouble was that Skipper Tipton was going to keep on running, too.

And Skipper had brand-new, bright blue shoes with silver arrows.

2

After P.E. class, Izzy fell in line for the water fountain. When her turn came, she gulped down huge mouthfuls of cold water.

Back in their classroom, it was time for language arts. Their classroom teacher, Mrs. Molina, looked impatient as the stragglers wandered in from the water break.

"All right, class," she said, once everyone was seated. "I want to tell you about our upcoming language arts assignment due next Friday, a week from today."

On the chalkboard she wrote two words: *Famous Footprints.*

Izzy copied the words onto a blank page toward the end of her language arts notebook. She liked the assignment so far, from the name of it. She liked anything to do with feet! And it was appropriate that the Famous Footprint report happened to be due on the same day that the third graders were having their Field Day.

"Each one of you will pick some famous person whose footprints you'd like to follow someday," Mrs. Molina went on. "If you'd like to grow up to be a scientist, you could pick a famous scientist like Marie Curie. If you'd like to be a musician, you could pick a famous composer like Beethoven."

Izzy could pick a famous runner!

Skipper would probably pick a famous runner, too.

Mrs. Molina continued. "You'll get a book from the library about your famous person and read it. The more you learn about your famous person, the more you'll know what you need to do to follow in that person's footsteps."

She held up a piece of paper on which she had traced around two large shoes to make the outline of two footprints.

"I have blank footprints here for everyone. When you're ready to do your report, you'll write some of the things you learn about your famous person inside these footprints. Then next Friday we'll hang all of them in the hall-way outside our room so that everyone can see what inspires each one of us to be the best we can be."

Simon raised his hand.

"What if our report is too long to fit inside two footprints? Can we write the rest of it on regular paper? Or on extra footprints?"

Simon's reports were always the longest and the best. Izzy giggled to herself as she imag-ined twenty or thirty footprints marching from

Mrs. Molina's room down to Mr. Boone's office to contain Simon's enormous report.

Mrs. Molina shook her head. "Just write enough interesting and important facts to fit inside the footprints."

Simon looked disappointed.

Cody raised his hand next. Cody's reports were always the shortest and the worst.

"Do we have to fill up both footprints?" he asked.

"I'm sure you can find enough material to fill two footprints, if your person is famous enough, Cody," Mrs. Molina replied.

Cody looked disappointed, too.

The class lined up to walk down to the library together. Izzy bounced in place as she stood in line between Annika and Kelsey. She liked going anywhere more than she liked sitting still.

At the library Mrs. Molina helped Izzy find a biography of a famous runner named Wilma

Rudolph. Izzy had never heard of Wilma Rudolph; Wilma had died before Izzy was even born. The back of the book said Wilma Rudolph had been the fastest woman on earth despite having a foot twisted from a disease called polio.

Izzy hugged the book. Mrs. Molina might be a strict teacher who didn't like long water breaks, but she knew how to find a good book.

She saw Skipper holding a book about another famous woman runner: Jackie Joyner-Kersee.

Izzy hoped that Jackie Joyner-Kersee wasn't a faster runner than Wilma Rudolph.

Annika found a biography of Albert Einstein; Einstein used a lot of math to make his scientific theories.

"Look at his hair!" Annika said to Izzy and Kelsey. In one picture, Einstein had the messiest hair Izzy had ever seen, long white wisps sticking out from his head in every direction. In another picture he was sticking out his tongue.

Maybe Albert Einstein was like Mr. Boone, silly on purpose to make people laugh.

Kelsey showed her friends the biography she'd found of Laura Ingalls Wilder, who had written the Little House books.

"What did you get?" Izzy asked Simon as they waited to check out their books.

Whose footsteps would Simon want to follow, given that he was a reading star, a math star, a science star, and a social studies star? He was even a running star, though not as starry on the track as Izzy and Skipper.

Simon held up his biography. Izzy wasn't sure how to pronounce the person's name.

Simon pronounced it for her: "Lee-oh-nar-do dah Vin-chee."

He was even a star at pronouncing long, unfamiliar words.

"Who's Leonardo da Vinci?" Izzy asked.

Simon looked amazed that anybody didn't know.

"He was a famous painter! He painted the *Mona Lisa*! And he was a famous scientist and a famous inventor! He thought up the idea of a helicopter hundreds of years before anybody else! He knew everything about the human body! He knew everything about everything!"

Oh.

It figured.

Cody, Izzy saw, didn't have a book to check out. He was in the hall by the water fountain getting a second drink even though Mrs. Molina didn't approve of second drinks. Maybe Cody wasn't going to follow in any famous footprints at all.

Izzy was glad she could read a book about a famous runner like Wilma Rudolph. No famous footprints were footprint-ier than a runner's footprints.

But even more than reading a book about a runner, she wanted to be outside running herself.

And running faster than Skipper Tipton.

3

On Friday nights Izzy's thirteen-year-old half brother, Dustin, arrived to spend the weekend with them. Dustin had the same father as Izzy, but he had a different mother. During the week he lived with his mom, but on the weekend he lived with their dad and Izzy's mom and Izzy. So from Friday night to Sunday night, she gained a brother. But lately she felt she lost a little bit of her father, too.

When she was younger, she used to love to watch all of Dustin's soccer games with her dad. But now, between softball and running, she had sports events of her own.

Even last year, her games had been kiddie games with no playoffs for an end-of-season championship. So she hadn't minded that her dad sometimes chose to go to Dustin's big, important games instead. Now Izzy's games were big, important games, too.

But however big and important her games and races were, Dustin's games always seemed bigger and more important. This season he had joined a traveling soccer team that played all over the state of Colorado.

"Dustin!" their dad said that evening, once the pizza man had dropped off their Friday-night pizza. They started every weekend with pizza: Dustin's favorite food. It was always pepperoni and sausage with green peppers and onions: Dustin's favorite kind of pizza. "So what's new with you this week?"

"Nothing," Dustin said, his mouth already full of his first huge bite.

Dustin definitely preferred eating to talking.

"Big game tomorrow!" their dad said. "Play-offs for the Lightning Bolts!"

That was Dustin's traveling soccer team, which had a home game this week.

"*Two* big games tomorrow," Izzy's mother reminded him. "Playoffs for the Jayhawks!"

That was Izzy's softball team. The end of May was playoff season for everyone.

"I wish I could be there," her mom told Izzy, "but I drew the weekend shift this time." Izzy's mother was a nurse at the hospital downtown.

Izzy wanted to ask her dad which game he was going to. She understood that he had to go to Dustin's away games, but her home games should count just as much as Dustin's home games. Right now, though, there was something else she wanted to ask him even more.

"Daddy?" she began as Dustin was still devouring his pizza.

"What is it, Izzy Busy Bee?"

"I need new running shoes."

A frown creased Izzy's mother's face. "Izzy, your shoes aren't even two months old!" she said. "There is no way they could be worn out yet, and you couldn't possibly have outgrown them this soon."

Izzy had known that was what her mother would say. She kept her pleading gaze on her father.

"Skipper Tipton has new shoes, and her old shoes weren't worn out or outgrown, either. Her dad bought them for her. He said they'll make her run faster, and a dad who's a running coach should know. And, Daddy, Skipper's shoes are so beautiful, blue with silver arrows on them, and I know I'd run faster with shoes like hers. I would!"

Izzy's father looked at his wife. She shook her head.

Then he looked at Izzy. She knew he wanted to give in.

"They can be for my birthday next year," Izzy offered. "And for Christmas, too."

Dustin washed down his third slice of pizza with half a glass of milk in a single gulp.

"Izzy's shoes are dorky," he said. "Skipper's shoes are cool."

Dustin had taken her side! He already had cool shoes; he had told their dad a few months ago that he needed them to play for the Lightning Bolts.

Please please please please! Izzy beamed the words at her dad. *PLEASE!*

"Your mother and I need to talk about this together," he finally said. "By ourselves. After dinner. So no more begging."

Her mother sighed.

Izzy knew that meant yes!

Inside her old dorky shoes, her toes tingled with anticipation. If she had shoes like Skipper's, she knew she could win the race on Field Day, and the 10K race, too. She would be a blue-and-silver bird that could fly forever.

An hour and a half later, Izzy sat with her dad and Dustin at the food court at the mall eating frozen yogurt: swirled-together vanilla and chocolate in a cup heaped with all kinds of toppings—strawberries, raspberries, M&Ms, broken pieces of peanut butter cups, gummy bears.

She couldn't keep her eyes off her feet in their blue-and-silver splendor.

"Thank you, thank you, thank you!" she told her father for the twentieth time.

She would wear her new shoes every day for the rest of her life—well, every day until they were too small for her to wear anymore. She'd never wear her dorky old shoes again. Izzy knew just what to do with her old shoes, too: she would donate them to the Franklin School shoe tree.

Franklin School was doing a weeklong drive to collect "gently used" shoes to donate to needy children around the world. The shoes were to be hung on a bare-branched tree standing in the front hallway of the school outside Mr. Boone's office, starting Monday. Her mother was right: Izzy's old shoes really were in excellent condition. Some child somewhere in the world who didn't need to beat Skipper Tipton could wear them happily.

Izzy savored a long, slow spoonful of her frozen yogurt. Now, if only her father would come to her softball playoff game tomorrow, and then come to Field Day, and *then* come to her 10K race, she would have everything in the world that anybody could ever want.

4

On Saturday morning Izzy's father was up early, making pancakes, scrambled eggs, and sausage links for Izzy and Dustin. Izzy's mother was already at the hospital for her twelve-hour shift.

"Gotta provide some good fuel for my two star athletes," Izzy's dad said as he set a platter of pancakes on the kitchen table. He never made pancakes during the week, because schoolday/workday mornings were too rushed.

Her father whistled as he slid a big helping of scrambled eggs onto Izzy's plate and an even bigger one onto Dustin's. He whistled more on the weekends, too.

Dustin stacked an enormous pile of pancakes on his plate and poured an enormous amount of syrup on top of them.

"Go, Jayhawks!" their dad said as he gave Izzy two plump sausage links.

"Go, Lightning Bolts!" he said as he gave three sausages to Dustin.

Izzy was afraid to ask the question, but she had to know the answer.

"So are you going to Dustin's game or mine?"

"Both! I'll start out rooting for the Bolts, and then at halftime I'll drive over to the softball field and root for the Hawks. How's that? I talked to Kelsey's mom; she's going to give you a ride to your game, since Kelsey and Annika want to come as your cheering section. Dustin has a ride home with one of his teammates, so we're all set. Just try not to hit any home runs until the fourth inning, okay?"

Izzy grinned at him. She knew her father re-ally wanted her to play her best all game long.

"I'll hit lots of home runs," she said, "but I'll save my super-duper-est home run until you get there."

As Izzy swallowed another delicious bite of pancake, Dustin reached over and speared one of her two sausages so quickly that she hardly saw him do it.

"Dustin!" she scolded.

He grinned at her with their father's grin; Izzy hoped she had that same grin, too.

"You weren't going to finish it, anyway," he said. "You never do."

Izzy's father replaced the stolen sausage on Izzy's plate and gave Dustin two more as well.

"There's no need to rob your sister's plate," he said, giving Dustin a playful whack on the shoulder and then gently tugging one of Izzy's short, tight braids. "There's plenty for both of you."

* * *

When Kelsey's mom pulled into the driveway to pick Izzy up for the game, Izzy didn't wait to see if her friends would notice her feet. As soon as she flung open the car door, she called out the wonderful news.

"Look at my shoes! My dad got them for me last night!"

"They're beautiful!" Annika said, even though Izzy knew Annika had never spent a moment of her life admiring running shoes.

"Take that, Skipper Tipton!" Kelsey squealed.

Izzy beamed. "I'm glad my dad picked to go to the first half of Dustin's game and the second half of mine. Watching the second half is better than watching the first half because that's when our team wins or loses."

"When your team *wins*," Annika corrected her.

Izzy gave both of her friends a high five.

As yesterday had been perfect weather for running, today was perfect weather for softball—not too hot, not too windy, not too anything.

Izzy was glad that Skipper wasn't on her softball team; Skipper was playing spring soccer instead.

In the first inning, Izzy caught a fly ball in the field and hit a single at bat.

In the second inning, she scooped up a ground ball and threw it to first base in time for an out. She got walked to first base but didn't have a chance to score a run.

In the third inning, she didn't have any fielding action and didn't get up to bat, either. It was good that her father hadn't hurried away from Dustin's game to see her doing big fat nothing.

In the fourth inning, she caught another pop

fly, but she also struck out. Izzy knew that even the greatest hitters in the history of baseball struck out more than they got on base—a lot more. Still, Izzy hated when she swung her hardest, three times in a row, only to connect with air. She was just as glad that her father hadn't raced there to see her strike out.

See, she could tell him later, *I did save my home run for when you could watch me do it.*

But scanning the bleachers as she took the field for the fifth inning, she still couldn't spot him anywhere. Nor was he there to see her leap for a hard catch in the sixth inning to retire the side, leaving the game tied 9–9.

Come on, Daddy! The game only has seven innings! It's going to be over before you get here!

In the top of the final inning, Izzy was so busy watching the parking lot next to the field to see if her father's car was pulling in that she

flubbed a catch and let the other team score two runs, increasing their lead from 10–9 to 12–9.

Izzy's coach, Coach Dan, one of the other players' dads, laid a comforting hand on her shoulder as she trudged off the field at the middle of the inning.

"Don't take it too hard," he told her. "Everyone can miss a catch now and then. You're a terrific outfielder. Just put this behind you and show them at your next at-bat."

Izzy tried to swallow the lump in her throat, but it stuck there and wouldn't go down.

She didn't let herself keep scanning the parking lot or the bleachers as she waited to come to the plate. By the time it was her turn, the score was 12–10, with two runners on base.

Izzy got a strike on the first pitch.

Concentrate!

Two balls next. She was proud of herself for watching them go by without taking a swing.

Then, on the next pitch, she swung and heard the sweetest sound in the world, the sound of a bat connecting squarely with a ball. *Thwack!*

As the ball soared into the outfield, Izzy tossed down the bat and ran.

Around first base.

Around second.

She thought she could hear Kelsey and Annika screaming, "Run, run, run, run, run!"

Around third.

The other team's outfielder had finally chased down Izzy's hit and thrown the ball to the pitcher, who threw it toward home.

Izzy ran even faster. She reached home plate right as the catcher grabbed the ball in her mitt. Or maybe a split second before?

"Safe!" she heard the umpire call.

The other Jayhawks were hugging her, screaming, pounding her on the back. They had won, 13–12, on Izzy's home run.

The crowd streamed down from the bleachers to add their hooting and hollering and hugs. Kelsey's mother hugged Izzy as Annika and Kelsey danced around her, shrieking. All the parents were shouting as loudly as the kids.

All the parents, except for Izzy's dad.

5

You're riding home with us," Kelsey's mother said. "Your dad texted to tell me he was running late, and I told him I'd take you with us if he didn't get here in time."

"Thanks," Izzy said, smiling as if it were completely fine that her father hadn't been there to see her winning home run.

At least Kelsey's mother hadn't said, *Too bad your dad couldn't make it.* Kelsey and Annika didn't seem to notice the absence of Izzy's dad at all. They were too busy talking about how amazing the end of the game had been.

"After that first strike I couldn't even look," Kelsey said. "I buried my face in Annika's shoulder and made her watch for me. Like when I'm reading a scary book, I can't make myself read the scary parts unless I peek at the ending to make sure it's all going to turn out okay."

"I kept reciting the times tables over and over again in my head," Annika said. "Seven times six is forty-two. Seven times seven is forty-nine. Seven times eight is fifty-six. To make me less stressed."

Kelsey stared at Annika. "That would totally make me *more* stressed!"

"Next time, try it," Annika recommended. "I had gotten up to nine times eight is seventy-two when Izzy hit the ball and started running. And then I couldn't do any more times tables. I just sat there chanting 'Run, run, run, run, run!'"

"Were you dying, wondering if you'd run all those bases only to be tagged out at the very last one?" Kelsey asked Izzy.

"Nope," Izzy said. "I knew I had to run faster than I had ever run in my life, so I did."

She wouldn't be able to run that fast for the Franklin School Field Day race or the 10K race. For those races, she'd have to pace herself so she wouldn't get burned out too quickly. But today, wearing her brand-new shoes, she had tried to run as fast as an Olympic sprinter, like Wilma Rudolph, who won her first gold medal in the 100-meter dash.

Izzy climbed into the backseat of Kelsey's mother's car, glad for the comfort of being sandwiched between her two best friends.

"Oh, wait," Kelsey's mother said. "Here's your dad's car now."

Izzy's dad's blue station wagon, its loud engine racing, pulled up next to Kelsey's mom's sedan and screeched to a halt. Slowly, Izzy unbuckled her seat belt and climbed over Annika.

"Bye, Izzy Barr, softball star!" Kelsey and Annika chorused.

"Congratulations again on a great game," Kelsey's mom said, her voice gentle. Even if she hadn't said anything out loud about Izzy's dad missing the game, Izzy could tell she was thinking it now.

Izzy closed the car door behind her, trying not to let it slam. Her father got out of his car and knelt down beside her, looking up into her unsmiling face.

"I'm sorry, honey," he said. But Izzy could tell that he misunderstood the reason for her scowl. "Losing a big game is always rough. But you Hawks should feel mighty proud of yourselves, anyway. Only four teams out of twenty even made it to the playoffs."

"We won," Izzy said, her voice flat and expressionless. "Thirteen to twelve. I hit the home run that made us win."

"And I missed it," he said sorrowfully. "Dustin's game started late because the other team's bus

broke down on the way, and then the Bolts were behind two to one at the half, and Dustin hurt his ankle, not bad enough for the coach to take him out of the game, but bad enough that I hated to drive off and leave him there. I guess I just figured that . . ."

Izzy wondered if he was going to finish the sentence: *. . . an eighth-grade soccer game is more important than a third-grade softball game.* He didn't.

"That's okay," Izzy said, then thought quickly. "It was even better! When I get up at bat and everybody's watching me, I get more nervous, and then I swing when I shouldn't, and I strike out. I probably wouldn't have hit that big home run if you had been there. Really."

Izzy could tell from her dad's face that he was relieved.

"Do you mean that, honey?"

Izzy nodded so vigorously that her braids bounced, too.

"Or running," she went on. "I run better when I don't have a lot of people staring at me. It's easier to concentrate."

Now that she had started, she couldn't stop.

"So I'll do better at Field Day on Friday if you don't come. Not that you could come anyway, because it's a weekday and you have to work."

Although she remembered that he had taken off from work once to go to an away game of Dustin's.

"And my 10K race? I'll run faster if you aren't there."

"Come on now, Izzy Busy Bee," her dad said then. "You did just fine when I was there at the 10K last year. You won't even see us in a crowd that big."

"Yes, I will! I always know when you're there!"

And when you're not there.

"Besides," her father added, "your mom has her heart set on seeing you run into the stadium at the end of your big race."

"Mom can still come," Izzy said. She noticed her dad hadn't said that *he* had his heart set on seeing her finish the race. "She doesn't make me as nervous as you do."

A shadow passed over her dad's face.

"She just doesn't."

For a moment neither of them said anything.

Her father broke the silence first. "Well, the 10K race isn't till Memorial Day. I won't come if you truly don't want me there, but tell me if you change your mind, okay?"

Dustin, who had been sitting in the front seat the whole time listening to music through his earbuds, opened his car door. "Are we going to get some burgers, or not?" he asked. "I'm starving!"

"I'm starving, too," Izzy said.

She didn't ask Dustin if his team had won. Right then she didn't care. She climbed into the backseat. Someone had to be the one to sit all alone in the backseat, and somehow that some-one always turned out to be her.

6

For the rest of the weekend Izzy tried to act happy.

She acted happy when she went to another friend's birthday party at the rec center on Saturday afternoon with Annika and Kelsey. At least Skipper wasn't there. Swooshing down the two huge waterslides, Izzy shrieked louder than anyone.

She acted happy when she went to a brunch buffet after church on Sunday with her dad, her mom, and Dustin. Dustin ate fourteen sausage links. He said he needed to keep up his strength for his soccer team's championship game next weekend; it was on the Western Slope of Colorado, a few hours' drive away. Dustin's game was the same day as the championship game for Izzy's softball team.

Izzy knew her dad had to travel with Dustin's team. But even if it had been a home game, he might have picked Dustin's game anyway. Dustin was practically in high school; Izzy had to admit that Dustin's games were super-exciting. Besides, her dad only got to see Dustin on weekends. *When Dustin is here, we'll play putt-putt*, her dad would say. *When Dustin is here, we'll all go on a family bike ride.*

It was a good thing she had told her dad she didn't want him to come to any of her games ever again.

Izzy kept smiling brightly as she left her last two sausage links uneaten on her plate.

She was glad when Monday finally came.

Kelsey's mother always drove the three friends to and from school because she was the only stay-at-home parent in the group. The first thing Izzy saw when Mrs. Green dropped them off on Monday was Mr. Boone jogging around the flagpole. He had traded his principal suit and tie for a bright green jogging suit with reflecting silver stripes that reminded Izzy of the silver arrows on her beautiful new running shoes. He had a matching green-and-silver headband, too.

"Good morning, Izzy—Annika—Kelsey!" Mr. Boone called out, making a big show of gasping for breath as he spoke.

"Good morning, Mr. Boone!" the girls called back, giggling. It was all right to laugh at Mr. Boone, because it was so clear he wanted them to.

"We have to go inside and put my old shoes on the shoe tree," Izzy told her friends.

The tree stood completely bare, ready to begin receiving donations.

"You're going to be the first one!" Kelsey said.

"Ahead of Skipper," Annika said.

"If she even donates her old ones," Izzy said. Maybe Skipper had a whole room in her house filled with her cast-off shoes: the Skipper Tipton Running Museum.

Izzy took her dorky shoes out of her backpack. Carefully, she knotted the laces together and hung the shoes over a branch halfway up the tree right in the front.

"Goodbye, shoes," she said. She gave them an affectionate little pat so they'd know she was grateful for all the happy miles she had run with them on her feet. But she was glad she had gorgeous new shoes to run with now.

After morning announcements and math, Mrs. Molina's class headed outside for P.E.

Izzy didn't say anything about her shoes to

Skipper or make a big show of tying and retying her laces a hundred times. But Skipper's
eyes fell on Izzy's feet right away.

"You got my same shoes!" Skipper cried.
"You copied me!"

Izzy wasn't sure what to say. She *had* copied
Skipper. But Skipper wasn't the only girl in the
school who could have new blue-and-silver
shoes in the nick of time for two big races.

Luckily, the warm-ups for the opening lap
around the track began. Today Skipper finished
the course one stride ahead of Izzy—maybe
Skipper's shoes were more broken in now. Cody
was only a few paces behind Simon, though
both boys finished a good distance behind
Skipper and Izzy.

"Cody's getting really fast," Annika said as
the girls walked from the track to the high-
jump pit. "I bet his time is just two or three seconds behind Simon's now."

Annika loved timing things in the same way she loved measuring things and counting things.

"Maybe Cody will beat Simon on Friday," Izzy said.

"Nobody ever beats Simon," Kelsey pointed out.

Well, Annika had beaten Simon in a sudoku contest once, but only because Simon had gotten too busy with all of his other activities even to enter. And Kelsey had tied Simon in a reading contest once, but she had had to read nonstop every day for a month to do it. So Kelsey was right: no one had ever competed directly against Simon in a contest and actually won.

Plus, Cody had never won anything. He was the worst in the class at reading, math, social studies, science, and paying attention to Mrs. Molina.

"Maybe you can give him some running tips," Annika suggested to Izzy.

"Maybe we can make up a cheer for him,"

Kelsey said. Kelsey loved to make up cheers. "Go—go—*Go*-dy. Go—go—*Co*-dy."

Izzy and Annika exchanged glances. Some of Kelsey's cheers were better than others.

"Okay, I'll keep on trying," Kelsey said.

Izzy cleared the high-jump bar easily on her first try. Annika cleared it, too, but Kelsey knocked it down.

"It's hard to jump and think up cheers at the same time," she explained.

At the start of language arts, Mrs. Molina gave Cody a stern look when he came in last of everyone from the water break. She gave him an even sterner look when he still didn't have a library book about a famous person for his Famous Footprint report.

"Where is your book, Cody?" she demanded.

Cody didn't answer.

"You did work on getting information about your person over the weekend, I hope."

Cody nodded.

"So where is it?" Mrs. Molina pursued.

"It's at home."

Mrs. Molina sighed.

Outside the open window next to her desk, Izzy could see Mr. Boone doing chin-ups on the playground bars for a group of second graders. He was as tall as the tallest chin-up bar, so he had to hold his feet off the ground as he struggled to chin himself.

"Izzy, you need to be reading your library book, not looking out the window," Mrs. Molina said.

"But Mr. Boone is—" Izzy began.

Mrs. Molina cut her off. "Mr. Boone doesn't have to write a Famous Footprint report by Friday. You do!"

It was too late. The rest of the class had already run over to the window to look.

"Children, back to your desks!"

Nobody left the window until Mr. Boone had

done a few more chin-ups. He definitely wasn't any better at chin-ups than he was at jogging. But he was definitely good at making second graders laugh. And at making third graders ignore Mrs. Molina's scolding.

"Now!" Mrs. Molina said, sounding even more cross this time.

Izzy made herself look away from Mr. Boone's antics and finish reading her Wilma Rudolph book. Of course, she didn't mind having to read about one of the greatest runners who had ever lived.

Wilma Rudolph was poor. Her parents were sharecroppers in a time when it was almost impossible for African Americans to get ahead.

Her family had twenty-two children. Twenty-two!

Worst of all, when she was four, Wilma had polio, a terrible disease that paralyzed hundreds of thousands of people in America, including

Wilma, who had to wear a horrible, heavy iron brace on her leg to walk at all.

But then, at age twelve, she decided to do whatever it took to walk without the brace she hated so much.

She learned how to walk again, and then she started to run.

And run.

And run.

Until one day she ran so fast that she became the first American woman to win three gold medals at the Olympics.

Izzy had looked up Jackie Joyner-Kersee on her parents' computer at home, and Jackie had won three Olympic gold medals, too. But Wilma Rudolph still had the best footprints ever.

7

On Tuesday afternoons Izzy had Fitness Club. On Tuesday evenings she had softball practice. Izzy loved Tuesdays.

Fitness Club didn't meet all year long, just in the spring, two afternoons after school each week: the whole point of Fitness Club was to train to run the huge 10K race on Memorial Day. Izzy knew she could beat her own time from last year: 55 minutes and 18 seconds. But the time she needed to beat wasn't her own time from *last* year: it was Skipper Tipton's time from *this* year.

It was strange that Mr. Tipton was Izzy's P.E. teacher and running coach in the Franklin School Fitness Club *and* the dad of the girl Izzy was trying her best to beat. Maybe this way Mr. Tipton would be happy whichever girl won. But he'd probably want his own daughter to win most.

Izzy did her warm-up exercises with the other kids in Fitness Club. Two other kids from Mrs. Molina's class, in addition to Skipper, were in the club, but not Annika, Kelsey, Simon, or Cody. Some parents were helping with Fitness Club, too, running alongside both the faster and slower kids so that nobody would be running completely alone.

Izzy wished her parents could help with Fitness Club, but of course they had to work.

Warm-ups completed, the Fitness Club took off running.

Izzy pressed herself to run faster than she

had last week, which was faster than she had run the week before that.

As she ran she could see Skipper's ponytail bobbing up and down with each step and Skipper's blue-and-silver shoes flashing. Thank goodness her own blue-and-silver shoes were flashing, too.

She thought how funny Mr. Boone had looked jogging around the flagpole.

She thought about Cody neck and neck with Simon in the P.E. race.

She thought how great Wilma Rudolph must have felt the first time she ran without the heavy brace dragging her down.

She tried not to think about her father and how he wouldn't be watching her cross the finish line on Monday. At least her mother would be there; her mother had the whole three-day weekend off for a change. But the race wouldn't be the same without her father.

Past the public library, past the little bagel place on the corner, past the park, Izzy ran.

On Wednesday Cody still didn't have a Famous Footprint book with him during language arts.

"Cody, the assignment is due on *Friday*," Mrs. Molina said wearily. "Two days away! You do have a book for the project at home, don't you?"

Cody hesitated. Then he shook his head.

Mrs. Molina glared at him. "Cody Harmon, I want you to go to the library right this minute and come back with a biography of some famous person whose footprints you want to follow. *Any* famous person."

Cody just sat there. For someone who was so fast at running around the track racing Simon, he was certainly slow at getting up from his desk to fetch a library book. Finally, sighing as heavily as Mrs. Molina herself, he headed off to the library while the rest of his classmates were busy taking notes from their library books to copy onto their footprints.

Cody was slow getting back from the library, too. At least he had a book with him now.

"Thank you, Cody," Mrs. Molina said with exaggerated politeness.

Izzy saw the cover of the book as Cody set it on his desk. It had a picture of an unsmiling, olden-day lady wearing a pearl necklace.

"Who is *that*?" Izzy whispered to Cody.

He turned the book so she could read the title: *Abigail Adams*.

Izzy had no idea who Abigail Adams was, except she was obviously a famous person from a long, long time ago.

Kelsey whispered the answer since Cody still hadn't said anything.

"Abigail Adams was one of the First Ladies. She was married to President John Adams."

Kelsey knew things like that from reading all the time.

Bewildered, the two girls stared at each other. *That* was the person whose famous footprints Cody wanted to follow?

But Cody must not have been all that eager to follow in the footprints of First Lady Abigail Adams, because he didn't open the book about Abigail Adams to read a single page.

After school at Kelsey's house, the girls finished their math homework, with Annika explaining some of the problems to Kelsey and Izzy.

"Are you nervous about Field Day?" Kelsey asked Izzy when they were done. "And about the big race on Monday?"

"A little bit," Izzy confessed. "I want to beat Skipper Tipton so much, and at the big race there might be some other girl who runs even faster than Skipper Tipton, so I might have to beat her, too, whoever she is."

And my dad isn't even going to be there to see me run because I told him not to come.

"How fast was the winning time for third graders last year?" Annika asked.

Izzy knew the answer without having to look it up: the scores of the top runners in each category were on the race website, and published each year in the newspaper, too.

"The winning time for nine-year-old females last year was fifty minutes, twenty-one seconds."

The 10K race sorted runners by age and gender, not grade level. Izzy and Skipper had both just turned nine, so they were in the same age group as well as in the same grade.

Annika scribbled some numbers on a piece of paper. "Let's call it fifty minutes to make the math simple. So all you basically have to do is run an average of two hundred meters per minute, and then run a little bit faster at the very end of the race. Do you want to borrow my new watch for the rest of the week to use whenever you run? It has a stopwatch on it, plus a pedometer that tells you how far you've gone, so you can time how fast you're running every step of the way."

"Sure," Izzy said.

Annika handed her the watch, and Izzy strapped it onto her wrist.

"I'll show you exactly how to use it," Annika promised.

"And don't get distracted by anybody or anything," Kelsey told Izzy. "There's a story about a famous maiden—that's another word for girl—in Greek mythology who was the fastest runner in the world. Like your Wilma Rudolph, Izzy, only longer ago. Her father wanted Atalanta—that was her name—to get married, but she didn't want to marry anybody because all she wanted to do was run."

Izzy liked Atalanta already. "So what happened?"

"She said she'd get married to a man only if he could beat her in a footrace," Kelsey continued. "Lots of guys raced her, and they all lost. But this one guy loved her so much that he went to get help from the Greek goddess of love."

"That doesn't sound very fair," Annika said.

"Don't blame me—blame the story," Kelsey said. "Anyway, the goddess gave him some beautiful golden apples. During the race, every time Atalanta got too far ahead, he rolled an apple out in front of her, and she slowed down to pick it up, and so he won, and they got married. The moral of the story is: Don't pick up any golden apples!"

"There won't be any golden apples at either of these races," Izzy said, wondering how Kelsey could possibly think this was useful advice.

"That's not the point! The point is not to be distracted by anything. Like if Skipper says something braggy, don't listen. And even if Mr. Boone comes along—on stilts, or riding a unicycle and wearing a clown costume—don't look. Don't look at the crowd, either, to see who's there watching you."

Or who isn't there.

Izzy decided she would remember Kelsey's story and wouldn't let herself be distracted by anything.

She held out her wrist to admire Annika's watch with its time-counting and distance-measuring buttons.

"You two are the best!" Izzy told her friends, beaming.

8

On the morning of Field Day, Izzy's father made pancakes for breakfast even though it was a weekday and Dustin wasn't there. Izzy's mom gave Izzy a kiss on her forehead as she got ready to head off to work. Her nurse scrubs today had flowers and flowerpots all over them.

"Good luck, sweetie," she said.

"Thanks!" Izzy said, over a mouthful of pancakes.

But she had something better than luck to help her win the third-grade race today. She had brand-new running shoes from her dad, Annika's stopwatch strapped to her wrist, and Kelsey's story still in her ears, plus inspiration from Wilma Rudolph. Her Famous Footprint of fascinating Wilma Rudolph facts was in her backpack, ready to turn in to Mrs. Molina that afternoon.

The only thing she didn't have was a parent to watch her win.

"How come you made pancakes even though Dustin isn't here?" Izzy asked her father, sopping up the last dribble of maple syrup from her plate with the last bit of pancake.

"I don't just make pancakes when Dustin is here," he protested.

"Yes, you do."

"I usually don't have time for pancakes on workday mornings. But this morning the factory isn't opening until noon because of a safety inspection, so I'm a gentleman of leisure."

He gave Izzy a searching look, as if there

was something he wanted to ask her, but then he turned away to flip another pancake.

A new idea popped into Izzy's brain.

If the factory was opening late, her father could come to Field Day! He had to know she hadn't meant it when she told him not to come. She couldn't make herself speak up and say that, but he had to know how much she always wanted him to be there. He was probably planning to surprise her.

Izzy felt her smile spreading as wide as the distance she'd leap today in the long jump.

"Do you want another pancake?" her father asked. "Or two or three?"

"No, thanks."

She couldn't run her best on a full stomach. But she could definitely run her best on a full heart.

* * *

Mrs. Molina didn't even try to make her class do any math between the end of morning announcements at eight-fifteen and the start of Field Day for all the Franklin School third graders at nine.

"We might as well go outside early," she said with a sigh.

Izzy cheered with the rest of her class.

Too excited to walk quietly in line, the boys, except for Simon, pushed and shoved as the class headed down the long hallway to the door that led out to the field. Partway down the hall, the boys, except for Simon, got into a contest to see how far they could kick their shoes off their feet. Half a dozen shoes went flying into the air, one of them narrowly missing Mrs. Molina herself.

Mrs. Molina, at the head of the line, whirled around in fury.

"Put those shoes back on!" she barked. "Field Day can still be canceled, you know."

Izzy knew that Mrs. Molina didn't really have the power to cancel third-grade Field Day. Not after Mr. Boone had been whipping everybody in the school into a frenzy of anticipation for the various Field Days for each grade all week. Izzy hadn't seen Mr. Boone anywhere this morning. Maybe he'd be outside on the field doing push-ups or sit-ups while he waited for the third graders to arrive.

"Boys!" Mrs. Molina said, even louder this time, as one more shoe soared through the air. "Put your shoes on *now!*"

The boys scrambled to retrieve their kicked-off shoes.

"Does everybody have his shoes?" Mrs. Molina demanded as she stood scowling back at the class. "If I see a single boy without his shoes, that boy will be spending Field Day in Mr. Boone's office. Am I making myself clear?"

She waited while the boys, except for Simon,

bent down to shove their shoes back onto their feet and retie their loose laces.

Izzy saw that one boy was still missing a shoe.

It was Cody.

"Where's your shoe?" Izzy asked in a low voice, dropping back to the end of the line to walk next to him.

"I can't find it," Cody said miserably. "And I can't tell Mrs. Molina because if she sees I don't have my shoe, she won't let me run against Simon in the race."

Izzy stared down at Cody's shoeless foot.

"How can she *not* see that you don't have your shoe? It's not on your foot!"

"I know. She might not notice if I don't tell her, but she's bound to notice if I do, and then I can't beat Simon."

As if Cody could beat Simon wearing only one shoe. Besides, sooner or later, Mrs. Molina noticed everything.

It wasn't Cody's fault that he couldn't find

his shoe. All of the boys, except for Simon, had kicked off their shoes. It was Cody's bad luck that he was the only one who couldn't find his to put back on.

"I'll tell her, and I bet she'll understand," Izzy said, sounding more confident than she felt. Mrs. Molina was often crabby. But on the morning of Field Day, with no time for math, and with the boys in her class kicking their shoes all over the hallway, she was even crabbier than usual.

Trailing outside behind the others, Izzy walked up to her teacher, who had sat down heavily on the bench at the edge of the playing field, while her class ran around whooping and hollering as if math had never been invented.

"Mrs. Molina?"

"Yes, Izzy?"

This was harder than she had thought it would be.

"*Yes*, Izzy?"

"It's Cody."

"What about him?"

"He can't find"—she had already started the sentence, so she had to finish it—"his shoe. He looked for it everywhere, really he did, but he just couldn't find it."

Mrs. Molina's gaze fastened on Cody, standing a short distance away, trying to hide his shoeless foot behind the other one.

Before Mrs. Molina could say anything, Izzy pressed on. "So I'm going to go back inside with him to help him look again, okay? If we don't find his shoe, he can't run in the race, and Cody *has* to run, he just has to."

Izzy wanted to add, *Because he has to beat Simon!* but she didn't.

Mrs. Molina's scowl softened. "All right. But remember, Izzy, the first event for our Field Day is the race around the track, and it's going to begin in ten minutes. Did you hear me? *Ten* minutes."

Izzy sprinted back inside the school, Cody loping crookedly behind her. She couldn't see a running shoe in the hallway anywhere.

"Could it have gotten kicked into an open door of one of the classrooms?" she asked.

Cody nodded. "Maybe. There was a lot of kicking."

Izzy looked in despair at the long row of doors extending down the corridor. She and Cody didn't have time to go into every single one asking whether anyone had seen a strange shoe come flying in. She couldn't even give Cody one of her old shoes from the shoe tree because Cody's feet were bigger than hers.

That gave her another idea. "Maybe it got kicked under the shoe tree!"

She and Cody hurried over to the shoe tree to look. Its bottom branches were so heavy with shoes they drooped under the weight, but no loose shoe was hiding beneath them. Izzy saw her old shoes again, now surrounded by shoes everywhere.

So where was Cody's shoe? A shoe couldn't just disappear, walking away on its own.

Then Cody's face lit up. "There it is!"

He pointed to one lone running shoe stuck on the very top of the tree, like a Christmas angel.

Like a very worn and shabby Christmas angel.

Cody's shoe was definitely the oldest shoe on the tree, with a visible hole where his big toe had pushed its way through the fabric.

"How could it get all the way up there?" Izzy marveled.

"I guess I'm pretty good at kicking," Cody said.

"You're good at kicking *and* running," Izzy told him.

How were she and Cody supposed to get it down? Neither of them could reach that high. If they shook the tree to dislodge Cody's shoe, dozens of other shoes would come raining down on them in a May-morning shoe-storm.

Maybe she could stand on Cody's shoulders, or he could stand on hers, and they could reach for it, trying not to knock over the entire tree. The tree already leaned too much to one side, from its uneven distribution of shoes.

Then Izzy heard a wonderfully familiar voice. "What's going on, Miss Izzy and Mr. Cody? Why aren't you outside for your Field Day?"

It was Mr. Boone, coming out of the front office.

And he was on crutches!

At first Izzy wasn't sure if Mr. Boone's crutches were part of his Field Day act: pretending to be out of breath, pretending to be wiping sweat from his forehead, pretending to limp from the exertion of his training. Pretending to need crutches from a training injury?

"No," he said sorrowfully, in answer to Izzy's

unspoken question. "I was hopping on the hoppy balls during first-grade Field Day yesterday morning to show the first graders what proper hopping looks like, and I hopped right off the ball and landed wrong on my foot. It's just a sprain, not a break, but the doctor said no more hopping for me for a while."

He made a sad face. But then he chuckled. And then he laughed so heartily that Izzy and Cody found themselves laughing with him, until Cody was clutching his side and Izzy's stomach hurt.

But they couldn't stand there laughing when the Field Day race was about to begin any second.

"That's Cody's shoe." Izzy pointed.

"And I need it," Cody said.

"Right now," Izzy finished.

"Ah," Mr. Boone said. "Well, crutches are no fun to walk on, no fun at all. But they happen to be very useful for retrieving stray shoes from high places."

Expertly, Mr. Boone hooked Cody's shoe off the shoe tree with his crutch and tossed it to Cody.

"Thank you!" Izzy and Cody shouted together.

Without waiting for Cody to put on his shoe, the two of them raced back outside, Mr. Boone hobbling along behind them.

9

The rest of the third graders were finishing their exercises as Izzy and Cody arrived. In a few seconds Cody had his shoe on and was warming up with Izzy.

Izzy thought she saw Mrs. Molina give a small smile.

As Izzy lunged first to her left and then to her right, she tried not to look at the group of twenty or thirty parents gathered at the side of the field. Most parents couldn't come to Field Day, of course, because they had to be at work at nine o'clock on a Friday morning. Kelsey's mom would be there, but not her dad. Neither of Annika's parents could come to school events on a weekday. Izzy's mother would be at the hospital.

And her dad?

Don't look, Izzy told herself sternly.

She wasn't going to be like Atalanta, so busy spotting golden apples in her path that she let herself get beaten in a very important race.

Luckily, the girls raced first, all the girls from the three third-grade classes.

"Ready!" Mr. Tipton called out, once the girls were in place at the starting line.

"Set!"

Izzy waited for the wonderful word she knew was coming next.

"Go!"

She took off like a cork from a bottle, exploding into motion.

Her strides long and even, her feet in her new

shoes springing with every step, Izzy took the lead. She didn't think about winning; all she thought about was running—how good it felt to be in motion, like a bird flying, like a rabbit darting, like a deer loping.

The pack of girl runners led by Izzy and Skipper, neck and neck now, rounded the stretch of track where the parents were gathered to watch and cheer.

Izzy couldn't resist stealing one peek. Her father would be hard to miss, taller than most of the other dads, wearing the old baseball cap he wouldn't let her mother throw away.

He wasn't there.

No tall man with a battered baseball cap was standing in the shade with the other parents.

Izzy swallowed the lump in her throat, as thick as a big, cold pancake that hadn't been cooked long enough.

Unable to summon the strength for a final

burst of speed, Izzy let Skipper reach the finish line a good ten feet ahead of her. Mr. Tipton was too busy timing the runners to give Skipper a fatherly hug, but he flashed his daughter a proud grin.

"Congratulations, Skipper," Izzy made herself say.

Skipper gave a smirking shrug, as if she won so many races that she couldn't be bothered to reply.

Annika and Kelsey were still finishing their lap around the track, so Izzy turned her attention to cheering for her friends.

"Go, Annika! Go, Kelsey!"

She tried to beam some needed energy their way, especially to Kelsey, who had slowed down to a walk. Finally, the girls' race was over. Kelsey and Annika both flopped down on the grass to rest.

Izzy ran to get her friends some of the cool

bottled water in the ice chest by the side of the field, grabbing a bottle for herself as well. It was good to have something useful to do.

"How can you still be running?" Kelsey wailed as Izzy returned with the three water bottles and stood jogging in place as she drank. Her feet itched for the chance to run the race against Skipper over again, this time running just a few seconds faster.

Now it was the boys' turn to take the field, and the girls' turn to watch and cheer.

Izzy hoped Cody's shoelaces were tied nice and tight. It wouldn't do to kick off any more shoes, not in the middle of a run.

She hoped he wouldn't slow himself down by peering behind him to see how Simon was doing—*if* Simon was behind him, that is, and not ahead.

She hoped he wouldn't remember how slowly he read and how many answers he got wrong in math.

She hoped he'd remember that he was the fastest boy in the whole third grade.

Except for Simon Ellis?

Simon took an early lead, as Izzy had done in the girls' race. Two boys from other classes were right behind him, and Cody was right behind them.

"Go, go, Go-dy!" Kelsey called out. "Go, go, Co-dy!"

Apparently she hadn't come up with a better cheer after all.

"Will Cody be able to catch up?" Annika asked Izzy. "Simon's pretty far ahead."

"Maybe," Izzy said. Skipper had managed to catch up all too well in the previous race.

Simon wasn't likely to let himself be distracted, but he might have started out too quickly, at a pace he wouldn't be able to sustain. Lots of times, the winner came from behind. But lots of times, the winner ran in the lead the whole way.

"I can't look anymore," Kelsey moaned. She sat down and hid her face in her hands.

"Eight times seven is fifty-six," Annika muttered. "Eight times eight is sixty-four. Eight times nine is seventy-two."

Simon held on to his lead. Cody had passed the other two boys; he still had a chance unless he stumbled or lost his shoe again.

"Cody, Cody, Cody!" Izzy shrieked her encouragement. Some of the other girls picked up the cheer: "Cody! Cody!" And then she thought she heard a deeper male voice joining in: "Go, Cody!"

It sounded like Mr. Boone, but of course a principal shouldn't cheer for one kid over another kid; a principal should cheer for all kids equally.

Izzy glanced behind her to see if Mr. Boone was cheering for Cody, but he was just standing there, leaning on his crutches, watching the race like everybody else. So maybe she had imagined it.

Cody was only steps behind Simon now. Izzy's legs tensed in sympathy, wishing they could sprint along with him. Her heart pounded as if she were the one running, not Cody.

He was so close! But not close enough. He needed a few more seconds to make up the distance, seconds he didn't have—

And then—

Cody's legs somehow jumped into an even higher gear.

One last impossible burst of speed—

And Cody won!

"He won, he won, he won!" Izzy shouted.

Annika broke off her muttered times tables. Kelsey uncovered her eyes, leaped up from the grass, and hugged both her friends. The whole class was hooting and hollering, including the boys who were still finishing their race.

Izzy looked at Mr. Boone again. He was beaming like the full moon lighting up the night sky. Kelsey liked to call him Mr. Moon.

Even Mrs. Molina was clapping, though maybe she was clapping for all the boys, to be polite. But when Izzy looked at her more closely, she saw that their stern, strict teacher had tears in her eyes.

10

Simon pushed his way through the crowd of kids high-fiving Cody.

"That was an amazing race!" he said sincerely, holding out his hand.

Simon was so good at everything, he was even a super-good good sport.

In the relay race, Izzy's team finished third—not bad considering that her team had Kelsey on it; Skipper's team was second. Izzy got a personal best in the long jump, but knocked down the high-jump bar on her second try; and she collected a blue ribbon for the softball throw.

Annika got a red ribbon in the high jump, which surprised her more than anybody. Kelsey didn't get any ribbons except for the yellow "participant" ribbon that every kid got, but she didn't seem to mind.

At the end of Field Day, after the closing hoppy ball race, everyone had Popsicles, even the parents. Izzy took a grape one, hoping its cool sweetness would melt that terrible raw-pancake lump in her throat.

It didn't.

After lunch, Mrs. Molina told her students to clear their desks and take out their Famous Footprint reports to share with the class.

"We won't have time for everyone to read his or her whole report, so try to pick just a *few* of your most interesting Famous Footprint facts to share." She looked over at Simon as she spoke.

"Then we'll have these on display in the hallway outside our room. Who would like to go first?"

Of course, Simon had his hand in the air before anyone else.

The two footprints on his paper were covered with the tiniest handwriting Izzy had ever seen. If an entire book on Leonardo da Vinci had been copied onto the soles of two ordinary-sized shoes, it would look a lot like Simon's Famous Footprint report.

"Just a few facts," Mrs. Molina reminded him. But Simon didn't need the reminder, since he always did what he was supposed to do anyway.

"Fact number one," Simon said. "Leonardo da Vinci had the ideas for a helicopter, a tank, a calculator, and solar power for energy four centuries before these things were actually invented."

Simon obviously had good eyesight in addition to good research skills.

"Very nice, Simon," Mrs. Molina said after he had read out two more Leonardo da Vinci facts.

Next she called on a girl who did her Famous Footprint on Eleanor Roosevelt and a boy who did his Famous Footprint on Babe Ruth.

Kelsey read from her Famous Footprint that Laura Ingalls Wilder didn't publish her first Little House book until she was sixty-five. Her books were translated into forty languages. An important award for a children's book author had been named after her: the Laura Ingalls Wilder Award.

Annika read that Albert Einstein discovered the equation $E = mc^2$. She tried to explain what it meant, but Izzy didn't understand it. Annika didn't explain why Einstein had such messy hair or why his tongue stuck out in his picture. Maybe the biography of Einstein didn't tell things like that.

When her own turn came, Izzy stood up and tried to read her Wilma Rudolph facts as loudly and clearly as Simon had read his facts about Leonardo da Vinci. Skipper had stumbled over a few words when she read her facts about Jackie Joyner-Kersee.

"Fact number one," Izzy said, since Simon had started off that way. "Wilma Rudolph had polio at age four and was told she'd never be able to walk again without a brace. Fact number two, she *did* walk without a brace. Fact number three, she *ran* without a brace and won three gold medals at the 1960 Olympics in Rome."

"Those are very inspirational facts," Mrs. Molina told her. "I can see why you'd want to run in Wilma's footsteps. All right, who hasn't had a turn yet?"

Cody was one of the few students who hadn't yet raised his hand. Mrs. Molina looked at him, then hesitated, as if she wasn't sure she should call on him and spoil his triumphant day. He was bound to have a terrible Famous Footprint: he had admitted he didn't have a book at home, and he hadn't even opened the biography he had dragged back from the library. But Izzy

could see that he had a completed Famous Footprint on his desk. She'd be willing to bet it wasn't about Abigail Adams.

"Cody?" Mrs. Molina asked.

Cody picked up his piece of paper. He hadn't managed to fill up two footprints the way Mrs. Molina had said they were supposed to, but at least he had something written on one of them.

"Mine isn't a Famous Footprint, because there isn't any famous person I want to be like when I grow up. So I couldn't do the assignment the way you wanted me to. I didn't do the famous part—I just did the footprint part, and wrote about someone I do want to be like someday."

Mrs. Molina adjusted her glasses. It was obvious she didn't know what to say. Library research was supposed to be an important part of the assignment. But writing about someone who truly inspired you was an important part of the assignment, too.

"My dad," Cody read aloud from his footprint. "My dad isn't famous. He works on our farm. He has another job, too. He drives a truck for the . . ."

Cody squinted down at his messy handwriting.

"For the county. He is a great dad. He coaches my soccer team. He goes running with me. He feeds our cats. He walks our dogs. He takes care of our pig, Mr. Piggins. When I grow up I want to be just like my dad. The end."

Everyone clapped, even though Cody hadn't done the assignment the way Mrs. Molina expected.

The lump in Izzy's throat came back again, even harder to swallow now than before. It felt like a whole plateful of pancakes stuffed into one huge bite.

Cody's dad had been at Field Day. Izzy had seen the big hug he gave Cody after his race.

Cody had the crummiest shoes of any kid in

their class, but he had his dad there to cheer him on.

Izzy would have done better running in old shoes, with her dad there to see her, than running in new shoes without him.

Besides, her dad had only bought her new shoes because Dustin had taken her side. For her dad, everything was always Dustin, Dustin, Dustin, and no bright blue shoes with silver arrows could ever change that fact.

Izzy slipped out of her seat and took the girls' room pass from the hook next to Mrs. Molina's desk.

"Can't you wait until language arts is over?" Mrs. Molina asked her. She hated bathroom breaks as much as she hated water fountain breaks.

Izzy shook her head.

"Well, go then," Mrs. Molina said.

Outside in the hall, Izzy walked as fast as she

could without running until she reached the towering shoe tree. She unlaced her new shoes and knotted the laces together. Then she took her old shoes off the tree and hung the new shoes in their place.

She was back in class a few moments later, her old shoes on her feet.

"That was fast," Mrs. Molina commented approvingly. A suspicious look crossed her face. "Is everything all right?"

"Sure!" Izzy said.

Her toes felt strange in her old cheap shoes after the springy spaciousness of the fancy new shoes from her dad.

"Everything is great!" Izzy said, blinking hard to keep back tears.

11

Kelsey was the one who noticed it first. The girls were sprawled on the floor in the family room at Kelsey's house after school, talking about how funny Mr. Boone had been at Field Day, whacking the hoppy balls with his crutches in pretend rage for making him sprain his foot.

"Your shoes!" Kelsey sat up and pointed at Izzy's feet. "What happened to your new shoes?"

Izzy shrugged.

"I thought you donated your old shoes to the

shoe tree," Annika said, her eyes following Kelsey's finger.

Both her friends waited for Izzy to say something.

"Stop staring at me! I just decided I liked my old shoes better, and they'd be, you know, good luck for the race on Monday. Because they've had more experience running."

"You took your old shoes off the shoe tree?" Kelsey asked. She made it sound like an accusation.

"So? They're still my shoes. The shoe tree has, like, a billion shoes on it. Besides, I didn't *take* my shoes. I *switched* them, and left my new shoes there instead."

"You *what*?" Annika asked.

Izzy wished her friends would stop making such a big deal about it.

"The new shoes made my feet hurt!"

Izzy willed her eyes not to fill up with tears.

Actually, the new shoes made her heart hurt, not her feet, but she was afraid she'd cry if she said that.

"Mom!" Kelsey yelled.

Kelsey's mother poked her head into the family room. "What is it?"

"Can you give us a ride back to school? We—well, Izzy—forgot something. Something really important. And we need to get it before the school gets locked up for the day."

Kelsey's mother gave Izzy an inquiring look. Izzy didn't say anything.

"Do you need a ride back to school, Izzy?" Kelsey's mom asked.

Izzy hesitated. She nodded.

Suddenly she remembered: today was the last day for the shoe tree! Today was the day that all the shoes were going away to the needy children.

"Then we'd better hurry," was all Kelsey's mother said.

When they reached Franklin School, Mrs. Green waited in the car while the girls pelted inside. The instant they came through the front door, Izzy saw that the shoe tree was bare. The tree itself was still standing in its place, one stray shoelace dangling from an upper branch like a leftover piece of tinsel. All the shoe ornaments were gone.

"Maybe the shoes are in Mr. Boone's office," Annika said, obviously trying to stay calm.

But the front office was closed. Kelsey tried the door, just in case. It was locked.

"They're just shoes," Izzy said in a small voice.

Just the beautiful new blue shoes with the silver arrows that her father had bought her because he knew she wanted them so badly. The shoes he would have seen her run in today if only she hadn't told him she didn't want him there.

Most of the classroom doors were shut,

lights turned off, teachers gone home for the three-day weekend. The only room that still had a teacher in it was Mrs. Molina's. She probably couldn't bear to leave until she had every last math paper graded.

Kelsey and Annika led the way, Izzy following behind.

Their teacher looked up from her desk, visibly surprised to see three of her students at school so late. She wasn't grading math papers; she was reading through the stack of Famous Footprints.

"The shoe tree is gone," Annika began.

"And we were wondering—" Kelsey said.

"If you knew where they took the shoes," Annika continued.

"Because Izzy's new shoes—"

"Got left on the tree by mistake—"

"Well, sort of by mistake—"

"And Izzy needs them—"

"For her big race—"

"On Monday," Annika finished.

Mrs. Molina reached under her desk and held up a pair of brand-new blue-and-silver running shoes.

"Are these your shoes, Izzy?"

Izzy stared at them. Then she grabbed them from Mrs. Molina and hugged them to her chest.

"I saw you were wearing your old shoes again," Mrs. Molina said. "And then I saw these on the tree, and I thought maybe there had been some kind of mix-up."

Mrs. Molina did notice everything!

The teacher smiled at Izzy, but then she turned back into strict, stern Mrs. Molina again.

"I must say that in all my years of teaching, I have never had a class who had so much trouble keeping their shoes on their feet!"

Izzy switched her shoes. She held out her old shoes to Mrs. Molina.

"Is it too late to put them with the other shoes from the shoe tree?" she asked.

"I will see that they get where they need to be," Mrs. Molina told her.

"Thanks, Mrs. Molina!" the girls chorused.

"Good luck on Monday," Mrs. Molina said. "Between Kelsey's reading, Annika's math, and your running, Izzy, the three of you have done a lot to make our class proud."

Grinning, the girls raced back to the car where Kelsey's mother sat waiting, reading her book.

"All set?" she asked them.

They beamed in response.

Izzy's feet felt so much happier now.

If only her heart could feel happier, too.

12

Izzy's softball team played their championship game on Saturday morning despite gusty winds that threatened rain. Her mom was there to see Izzy hit one double and two singles. No home runs, but Izzy knew she couldn't hit a home run in every game. She knew the Jayhawks couldn't win every game, either. They lost this one, 12–10.

"I hate that other team!" Kelsey said after she had come running up to hug Izzy.

"I hate the umpire!" Annika said. "I think you were safe that one time when the umpire said you were out."

Kelsey and Annika didn't understand about sports. Izzy didn't hate the other team, or the umpire, or anybody. Her team had played their best. The other team had just played a little bit better.

Her dad called them from the Western Slope midday to hear Izzy's score and tell them that Dustin's soccer team had won 3–2. Dustin had kicked the winning goal. They had decided to stay overnight to do some father-son sightseeing, and they'd be home Sunday evening.

Izzy took one last training run on Saturday afternoon. Usually she did long weekend runs with her father or Dustin. This time she ran alone, around and around the few blocks of her little neighborhood.

It had started raining, but Izzy loved to run in the rain. No one else was out except for some people walking dogs. Maybe the dogs also loved the rain. As she ran, Izzy lifted her face up to the sky to feel the cool drops streaming down her face like tears.

Today she didn't even bother to monitor her time and distance with Annika's borrowed watch. Today she needed to think about something else.

She had her running shoes back, thanks to Kelsey, Annika, and Mrs. Molina.

Now she needed to fix things with her father. This time she had to do it all by herself.

Wilma Rudolph had wanted to run without a brace, and she had done it. The hardest part, harder than all the intense years of training that followed, had been taking that very first step.

Izzy needed to force herself to take the first step toward making things right with her dad. But how?

* * *

It rained hard all day Sunday. Izzy hadn't planned to run anyway; it was good to rest the day before a race. Her mother drove her downtown to pick up her race packet, which contained her racing bib, timing tag for her shoe, and souvenir T-shirt. Izzy spent the rest of the afternoon admiring how they looked laid out on her bed.

The house was quiet without her dad or Dustin. Izzy's mother made spaghetti for supper. It was good to eat a lot of carbohydrates the night before a race, too.

"Your father and Dustin don't have much time together," her mother said as they carried their plates to the table.

"I know," Izzy said.

"It's hard for Dustin having to live in two houses, without his dad during the week, without his mom during the weekend," Izzy's mother went on.

"I know," Izzy said again.

And she did. She really did.

The morning of the race, it was still raining.

"You don't think they'll cancel it, do you?" Izzy's mother handed Izzy the breakfast she had requested: two scrambled eggs and one piece of toast. Izzy's dad and Dustin were still asleep because they had gotten in so late the night before. Dustin was staying an extra day because of the holiday weekend.

"Of course not!" Izzy said.

One year Memorial Day had been swelteringly hot; another year it had been so windy that runners feared being blown off course. But the race was run in all kinds of weather. Tens of thousands of people came from all over just to run.

Izzy's mother was going to drop Izzy off at the start of the race and then come back later to the stadium, where the race came to an end. With a 10K race, people couldn't watch you run the whole race unless they were running along with you. It wasn't like a softball game, where you could sit in the bleachers and see the action from start to finish.

Izzy couldn't eat the rest of her eggs. Her stomach felt too jumpy and jittery to have eggy things bouncing around in it.

She tightened the laces on her shoes.

She strapped Annika's watch onto her wrist and set the time and distance features.

She tucked Kelsey's note into the top of one of her socks: "Don't look at any golden apples! Love, Kelsey."

Izzy knew she couldn't expect her friends to be at the stadium to see her, not after they had already given up half of Saturday watching her softball game, and especially not in terrible weather like today. Kelsey would be at home cozily reading. Annika would be at home cozily doing sudoku or playing with her dog, Prime. It was one thing to run in the rain; it was another thing entirely to get soaked through to the skin watching someone else run.

"Ready?" Izzy's mother asked her.

"Almost."

She took the note she had written for her father and put it on the kitchen table.

Dear Daddy,
    Please come to my race. I want you
to be there.

                                Love,
                                Izzy

On the envelope she had written DADDY in big bold letters. There was no way he could miss seeing it.

If he got up in time.

She suddenly remembered how her father loved to sleep in sometimes on mornings he didn't have to work.

Maybe she should tell her mother, *Don't let Daddy sleep too late*, but something stubborn in Izzy wouldn't let her say it.

She checked the envelope one last time to make sure it was right in the middle of the table, with the word DADDY facing up.

"Okay," she told her mother. "I'm ready now."

13

The race was organized into "waves" of runners scheduled at different times, so that tens
of thousands of runners wouldn't be crammed
together as they ran. The winners in each age
group were the ones who finished with the
fastest times, whichever wave they happened
to be in. Izzy's assigned wave was fairly early,
starting at 7:30 a.m. No wonder her father and
Dustin were still sleeping.

Already there, in the same crowded wave of
runners, Izzy found Mr. Tipton and Skipper. Except for the waves of the very fastest runners,

who had to qualify with a time from a previous race, you were assigned a wave based on the time you had said on your registration form that you expected to finish. So Izzy knew that she and Skipper were going to be running together.

Izzy fastened her timing tag on her shoe and forced herself to give Skipper a friendly smile. The other girl's smile was decidedly chilly. But the rain was chilly, too.

The race began.

Izzy started off too quickly; she knew she had. It was so hard not to want to pull ahead of Skipper right away. But she wanted to be a strong-finishing Cody, not a petering-out Simon.

She made herself slow down until Skipper and her dad had caught back up with her again.

"Good job pacing yourself, Izzy," Mr. Tipton told her.

Izzy could tell that Skipper didn't like it when her dad gave a compliment to his own daughter's rival.

Side by side, the three of them kept on running.

Had Izzy's dad gotten up in time to see her note?

No! Izzy wasn't going to be like Atalanta; this time she wasn't going to let herself be distracted by anything.

Last year Izzy had pounded past volunteers handing out cups of water and Gatorade, jugglers on unicycles, and cheering kids waving flags. She had thought the rain would keep the crowds away this year, but she saw plenty of people who didn't seem to mind the weather. Still, Izzy was glad her friends weren't huddled there shivering beneath dripping umbrellas.

At each mile marker, she checked the time on Annika's borrowed watch to make sure she was pacing herself correctly. She was actually running faster than she had planned—too fast? But she felt more confident, seeing Skipper and Mr. Tipton running right there beside her.

Forty minutes into the race, Izzy's feet still felt fine in her new running shoes. Her breath was steady; she didn't feel winded the way she'd felt last year when she'd had to run in a later wave in the hot morning sun. Her calf muscles throbbed, and her side ached a bit. She hoped she wasn't going to get a cramp just when she needed all her energy for a final spurt.

Was it time? She wanted to step up her pace, but if indeed it *was* time to pull ahead, why wasn't Mr. Tipton telling that to Skipper?

They were nearing the stadium. Now had to be the moment for Izzy to make her move and pull ahead of Skipper. And it was also the moment for Skipper to make her move and pull ahead of Izzy.

Her energy ebbing after running over six miles already, Izzy tried to pick up her pace and outdistance Skipper. But as she pushed herself to run faster, Skipper ran faster, too.

Izzy could see the entrance to the stadium.

Pretend you're Wilma Rudolph!

Pretend you've taken that heavy brace off your leg and now you can run, run, run, run, run!

With a final burst of speed, Izzy took the lead. She didn't glance back to see how big of a lead it was.

Pretend your dad is running next to you!

Pretend your dad is in the stadium waiting to see you win!

Then Izzy stopped pretending to be anybody else but Izzy Barr, doing anything but running her very best all by herself. No longer tired, muscles no longer sore, Izzy sprinted through the tunnel into the stadium and crossed the finish line.

Ahead of Skipper Tipton.

She had done it.

The rain didn't feel cold and dreary now. It

felt like a fountain spraying jets of celebration onto her upturned face.

She turned around to shake Skipper's hand, but Skipper was busy pulling her father away, obviously trying to avoid her. Apparently, Skipper Tipton needed some sportsmanship lessons from Simon Ellis.

"Izzy!"

Was that Mr. Tipton, calling after her?

It was. "Great job, Izzy! You did Franklin School proud."

"Izzy!"

She heard female voices calling her, too. She looked around to see where the cry had come from.

"Over here!"

Izzy saw them and started running—as if the 10K race had just begun—across the stadium, to where they had all come down on the field to wait for her: Annika, Kelsey, her mom, Dustin.

And, with the biggest smile of all, her dad.

Jumping up and down with excitement, Annika and Kelsey were holding up both ends of a huge, drooping, soggy banner that said, IZZY BARR, RUNNING STAR.

"We made our first sign out of cardboard," Kelsey said.

"Before we knew it was going to be raining," Annika chimed in.

"So we had to make it again," Kelsey continued.

"Out of fabric," Annika finished. "With waterproof markers so it wouldn't run."

Actually, the letters had still gotten awfully streaked and blurry.

Izzy thought they looked beautiful.

"Great race, little sis!" Dustin said. "Man, you came zooming into the stadium like a flying squirrel!"

Dustin wasn't one for hugging, so he gave her a brotherly whack on the back.

"You must be freezing," Izzy's mom said,

sweeping her into a hug. Her mother *was* one for hugging. "Let's get you into some warm, dry clothes, and then we can all go out and celebrate your fastest time ever."

It was true. Annika's borrowed watch said Izzy had finished her race at 52:12, three minutes and six seconds faster than she had run that distance the year before.

She wouldn't know until the scores were posted online after the entire race was completed whether she had beaten every other girl in her age group. Right now she didn't even care.

She had beaten Skipper.

And her father was there.

When her mother released her, it was finally her father's turn for a hug.

"I should have come to see you hit the winning home run at your ball game," he said into her ear. "And I should have checked again to see whether you really didn't want me to come to Field Day. I was wrong both times, and I'm sorry."

"I shouldn't have told you I didn't want you to come," Izzy said into his chest as he bent down his head to hear. "I always want you to come to everything!"

"Well, now we can both do things the way we should," he said. "Starting with a humongous, super-duper, big blowout celebration to end all celebrations! Where do you want to go?"

"Home!" Izzy said, standing back and flinging her arms wide. "For sausages and pancakes, and more sausages and more pancakes. Can Kelsey and Annika come, too?"

"You bet they can," he said. "Sausages and pancakes coming right up!"

Then Izzy and her father hugged each other again.

Fun Running Facts

Olympic running events come in many lengths, from the shortest (100 meters) to the longest (the marathon), and many lengths in between (200 meters, 400 meters, 800 meters, 1500 meters, 5000 meters, and 10,000 meters).

The marathon race (26.2 miles) is named after the city of Marathon, Greece. Legend has it that in 490 B.C., a messenger ran from Marathon all the way to Athens to report on whether the Athenians had won or lost a great battle against their enemies, the Persians. "Victory!" the messenger gasped out when he arrived. Then he collapsed and died. But no one knows if this is really true.

Begun in 1897, the Boston Marathon is the world's oldest continuous annual marathon. It is always held on Patriots' Day in April, the date of the first battle of the American Revolution. In the 2014 Boston Marathon, the oldest runner to finish the course was eighty-one years old; the youngest runner was eighteen.

Some races are over very quickly. The world record for the 100-meter dash is 9.58 seconds, set by Jamaican runner Usain Bolt. As famous runner Jesse Owens once said, "A lifetime of training for just ten seconds."

For decades people believed that no human runner could ever run a mile in under four minutes. But today the record for running a mile is held by Hicham El Guerrouj of Morocco, who ran a mile in just over 3 minutes and 43 seconds.

44.6 million pairs of running shoes were sold in the United States in 2012, for a total of over three billion dollars in sales.

The fastest running animal on earth is the cheetah, with recorded speeds up to seventy-five miles per hour, three times faster than a human being can run.

Many people enjoy running with their dogs. Some of the most popular breeds for a running companion are border collie, dalmatian, Jack Russell terrier, and German shepherd.

Acknowledgments

I'm grateful for the chance to thank just a few of the people who helped Izzy run her race to publication. My brilliant editor, Margaret Ferguson, worked with me to shape the entire Franklin School Friends series from the beginning. Her penetrating editorial comments make every book I do with her immeasurably better. I received careful critique on early drafts from my longtime Boulder writing group (Marie DesJardin, Mary Peace Finley, Ann Whitehead Nagda, Leslie O'Kane, Phyllis Perry, and Elizabeth Wrenn). Wes Adams read the manuscript with the eyes of a runner and had many helpful suggestions that found their way into the book; Susan Dobinick's editorial insights have been most welcome as well. Rob Shepperson's absolutely darling illustrations are my own favorite part of each Franklin School Friends title.

Thanks also to my wise and caring agent, Stephen Fraser; sharp-eyed copy editor Janet Renard; and Elizabeth H. Clark for the enormously appealing design of the entire series. Finally, my dear friend and accomplished marathoner Caolan MacMahon graciously answered all my questions about a runner's training and discipline; she is my inspiration for Izzy's joy in running.